STO

**FRIENDS
OF ACPL**

W9-BRL-218

ALLEN COUNTY PUBLIC LIBRARY

3 1833 00700 6130

Factual information for curious young minds, designed for inde-
pendent reading with 98% of the text in words from the Combined
Word List for Primary Reading

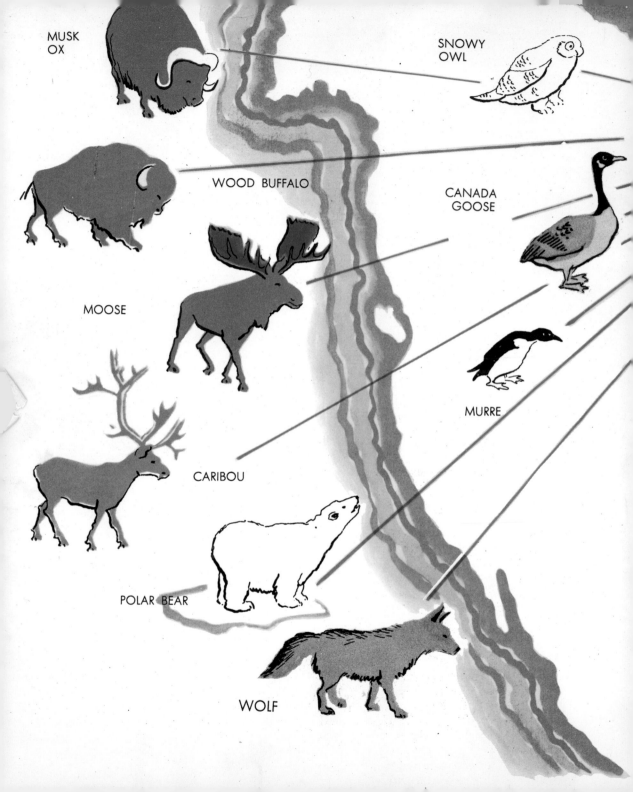

MUSK OX

SNOWY OWL

WOOD BUFFALO

CANADA GOOSE

MOOSE

MURRE

CARIBOU

POLAR BEAR

WOLF

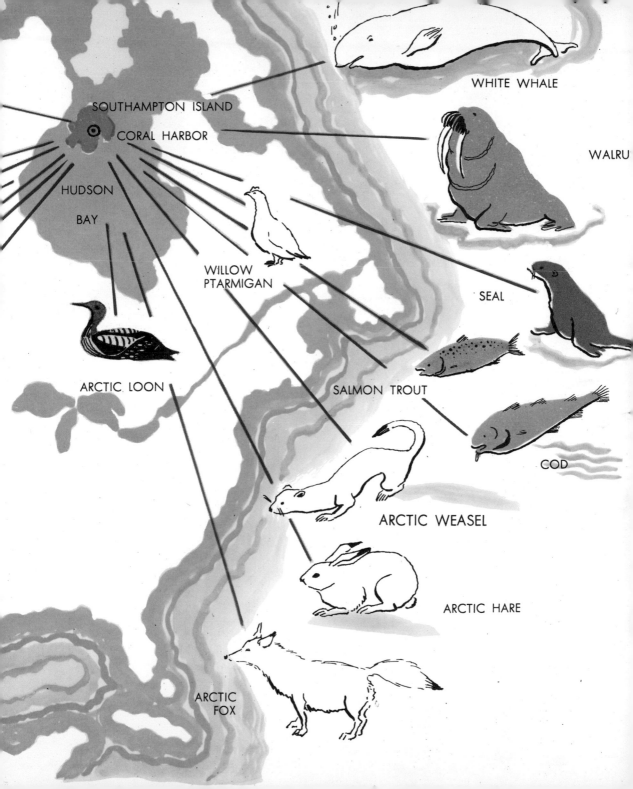

WHITE WHALE

SOUTHAMPTON ISLAND

CORAL HARBOR

WALRU

HUDSON

BAY

WILLOW
PTARMIGAN

SEAL

ARCTIC LOON

SALMON TROUT

COD

ARCTIC WEASEL

ARCTIC HARE

ARCTIC
FOX

the true book of

Little

Eskimos

by Donalda McKillop Copeland
pictures by Mary Gehr

CHILDRENS PRESS, CHICAGO

* To the "Toota" and "Amak" of
Southampton Island
and all the
Eskimo children of
Coral Harbor Federal School
and their teacher

COPYRIGHT, 1953, CHILDRENS PRESS. PRINTED IN THE U.S.A.

CO. SCHOOLS
C447733

Amak is a little Eskimo
boy. He lives with his daddy and mama and
brother and sisters in the far Northland.

In the summer time they live in a tent near the sea. The tent is made of deerskins, sewn together.

Amak is a happy little boy. He plays all day long with his sister, Toota.

Toota and Amak do as they please. No one ever scolds them. No one ever says "don't" or "no" to them. No one needs to—for most of the time, Eskimo children are good little ones.

Summer time in the far, far Northland is very short but it is beautiful.

The grass is the greenest green. The flowers are small and tender and very pretty.

But best of all the sun shines and shines, almost all the time. It never seems to get tired, for it never rests. It fills the sky with all the beautiful shades in the rainbow.

During the long summer days, Amak and Toota skip over the rocks. Sometimes they hunt for the little field mice called *lemmings*.

Often Toota takes along her rag doll that her mother made for her.

Always Toota and her brother are dressed in bright colors, for Eskimos love gay, pretty things.

KOMIKS

PARKA

All summer the mama Eskimo works getting warm clothes ready for the cold winter time.

She must chew and chew the heavy sealskin to soften it. Then she will make nice, soft *komiks* to keep little feet warm.

She must scrape and scrape deerskin to clean it. Then she will make fancy warm shirts with hoods on them, *parkas*.

Mama Eskimo works and works. But she never complains. She is always smiling and happy, too.

12

Baby Eskimo rides in the hood on the mama's back. He is really "King of the North." Sometimes his sister wants to ride, too.

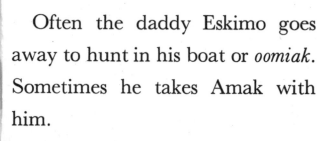

SEAL SPEAR

HUDSON BAY HARPOON

Often the daddy Eskimo goes away to hunt in his boat or *oomiak*. Sometimes he takes Amak with him.

Eskimos eat lots and lots of meat. They must hunt and hunt.

Amak knows that some day he must learn to hunt the walrus and the white whale and all the other animals that live in the Arctic seas.

They take along their big spear and harpoon and gun. Now they are ready for whatever they can find.

Soon they are out in the wide open sea—far, far from home. Here large pieces of ice float around in the chilly water. It is shivery cold even if it is summer time.

"What is that I see?" says the daddy Eskimo. "It is a great white polar bear on a cake of ice!"

"And there is another one in the water!" cries Amak.

Very quietly they row closer to the huge white creatures.

"Bang, bang," goes the big Eskimo's gun. Down

in a heap falls the big white polar bear.

"Bang, bang," goes the gun again. But it is too late. The other polar bear swims rapidly away.

Amak and his daddy hurry over to the "catch." They spear the enormous polar bear. Then they tie him to the boat.

"What a day," says Amak and smiles happily.

MOUNTAIN AVENS

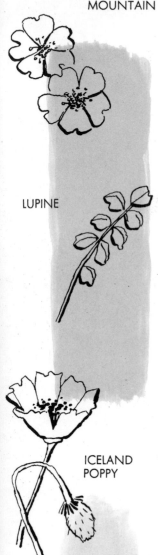

LUPINE

ICELAND
POPPY

ARCTIC
OXEYE DAISY

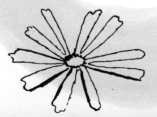

SAXIFRAGE

When Amak is away Toota goes to the hills to pick flowers. Sometimes her small brother and sister go with her.

Sometimes she takes along her rag doll whose name is *Pooka*.

All day long the children play among the rocks. Baby brother is just learning to walk.

There are so many different kinds of flowers, and they are all so pretty. But Toota likes the daisies best of all. They are so bright and cheery.

Summer in the Northland is so very short. She must enjoy every minute of it. So she spends her waking hours out of doors.

Soon summer is over!

The skies become gray. The wind blows and the snow begins to fall. All night long the wind howls and packs up drifts of snow.

Next morning Amak awakens suddenly. He hurries to the tent door. He sees the ground covered with beautiful white snow.

He awakens Toota and Poodlat. "Come quickly," he shouts, "the snow has come!"

The two little girls hurry into their clothes.

Then they all scurry outside.

The snow is falling in large, soft flakes.
The children join hands and sing:

Hurrah for the ice and snow
Hurrah for the winds that blow.

They are so glad that winter has come. They love winter time best of all the year.

The snow piles higher and higher.

"Now we must build an igloo," says the Eskimo daddy.

So the big Eskimo takes his snow knife and cuts a huge circle in the snow. Amak helps him with his small snow knife.

Then they cut out huge blocks of snow, just the right size and shape. These they fit together— up, up, up—and smaller and smaller, until they form a smooth round roof.

Amak and Daddy walk over the top of the snow house to see if it is strong enough.

"Now we have a nice warm igloo for the cold,
cold winter," says the mama Eskimo.

Daddy hurries to fill up the holes and cracks
with snow.

Mama hurries to line the walls and floors and
sleeping board with nice warm skins and fur.

That night everyone is happy and snug in the nice new igloo.

And outside, the Northern Lights glow in the frosty night.

As the days go by, the ice on the sea becomes harder and harder.

Sometimes Amak walks out on the ice to catch fish. He walks a long way from home. He takes along his spear.

First he jabs the ice with his spear, over and over again, to make a hole.

Then he waits and waits. Sometimes he waits a long time.

Finally he sees a fish. Quick as a flash, down goes the spear. It is so fast, the fish never know what happened.

Then Amak takes the fish home. Some, he puts in the meat pit to save for another day.

Then he gives all his Eskimo neighbors some, for Eskimos share everything.

The rest, Amak and his family eat that night. They eat and eat! And they drink cups and cups of tea. Everyone is happy.

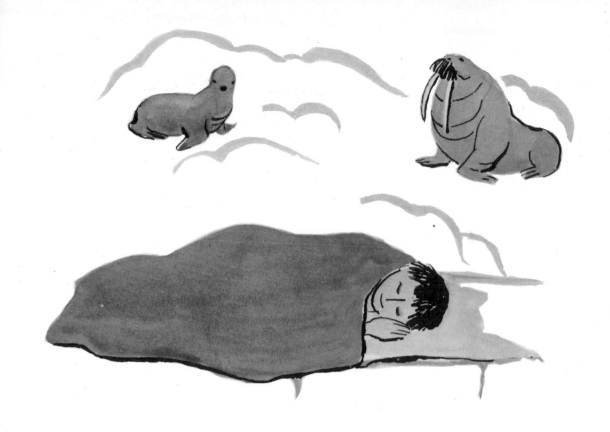

Amak dreams sweet dreams. He dreams of the icy sea and a fat seal and a walrus. He dreams all the long night for now the nights are long and the days are short. The sun is having its long winter rest.

The very next day the daddy Eskimo takes out his big sled or *komatik*.

He mends the broken cross bars. He draws new rope through the runners and over the cross bars.

He puts mud on the runners. Amak and Toota help him. Then they put water on the mud and rub it with a piece of bearskin to make it smooth.

"Now it will run swiftly and smoothly," says Amak.

"Tomorrow we go to hunt more meat for food," says the Eskimo daddy.

That night they go to bed early. They must not be tired for the long journey ahead.

The next morning, Amak and his daddy awaken early. They pack up bearskins to sleep on and enough meat for themselves and the dog team.

They take along a spear, harpoon, gun and large snow knife.

Then they harness the dogs, putting Kimik, the lead dog on the longest tie.

Now they are ready! No one says "good by"

for that is bad luck in Eskimo land.

"Wah!" shouts the Eskimo daddy, and he snaps his long whip in the air.

Away they go! Down the hill they fly, faster and faster until they are far out of sight.

Who knows how long they will be gone? Many many "sleeps," maybe.

They ride for many days. Each night they build an igloo for themselves and a snow shelter for their dogs.

Finally one day, they trap the cunning white fox. He is smart and hard to catch, but daddy Eskimo is smarter.

CO. SCHOOLS
C447733

The next night Amak shoots a
snowy white owl and a fluffy white
Arctic hare.

How proud he is! Brave little hunter.

"Ho-Hee," says the daddy Eskimo,
"now let us go to the sea."

So off to the sea ride the two brave hunters.

They ride many, many miles. Up over hills, down through valleys, over the ice and over the snow. At last they come to the sea.

It is much swifter riding now, for the ice is very smooth.

Over the ice they ride. Soon they come to a hole in the ice.

Amak and his daddy get off the sled. They hug the ice as they crawl closer and closer to the hole.

They wait and wait.

Soon a fat gray seal pops out, then another. Still another pokes his head out, for air and to have a look around.

Zing! Zing! Zing! goes the harpoon of the Eskimo hunter. Three dark heaps lie on the ice.

"Now we have plenty of meat," says the daddy Eskimo. "We must go home."

After many days they arrive home. All the Eskimos rush out to see them. They shake hands and rub noses. The tired hunters are happy. Everyone is happy.

Mama Eskimo was surprised and pleased when she saw the mighty meat catch.

"Hoo-Hee," says she. "Tonight we will have a feast. We will invite all the Eskimos."

"We shall tell brave hunting stories and sing brave hunting songs," says the big Eskimo daddy.

"And dance and dance!" says Amak.

"And eat and eat," says Toota.

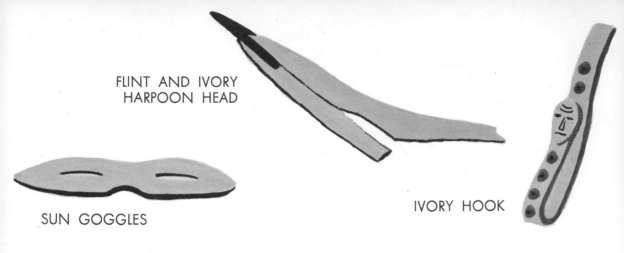

FLINT AND IVORY
HARPOON HEAD

SUN GOGGLES

IVORY HOOK

So this is the way Amak and Toota and other little Eskimos live.

Every night they romp and play in the igloo. Or they listen to daddy tell hunting stories.

Sometimes they play an Eskimo game. Sometimes they work. Often the daddy works on a new spearhead.

But always everyone is happy.

Every night Amak and Toota listen and watch. They begin to nod and yawn.

Soon they jump into bed, after prayers have been said.

IVORY SCRAPERS
FOR PREPARING SKINS

In a wink, they are fast asleep underneath the
fur blankets in their cozy little igloo near the
North Pole.

They dream of a feast, with lots to eat and
everybody laughing and happy.

Outside the igloo, the magnificent magic lights of the Northern sky snap and crackle and glow in rainbow colors in the silent night.

Everywhere on the snow, the lights make strange, wonderful shapes in the dark of the long Arctic night.

This is the story of Amak and Toota. And it is the story of every little Eskimo boy and girl, wherever you go in the far, far Northland.

Amak and Toota enjoy hearing stories of the strange white man. They like to hear about cars and trains and things they never have seen.

They rock with laughter when they learn that the funny white man sometimes gets his meat out of a small tin can!

But Eskimo children are happy and friendly. And Amak and Toota smile down on you from their northern igloo home.

They are your Arctic friends!

"Ee--eee," they say, which means, "Yes!"

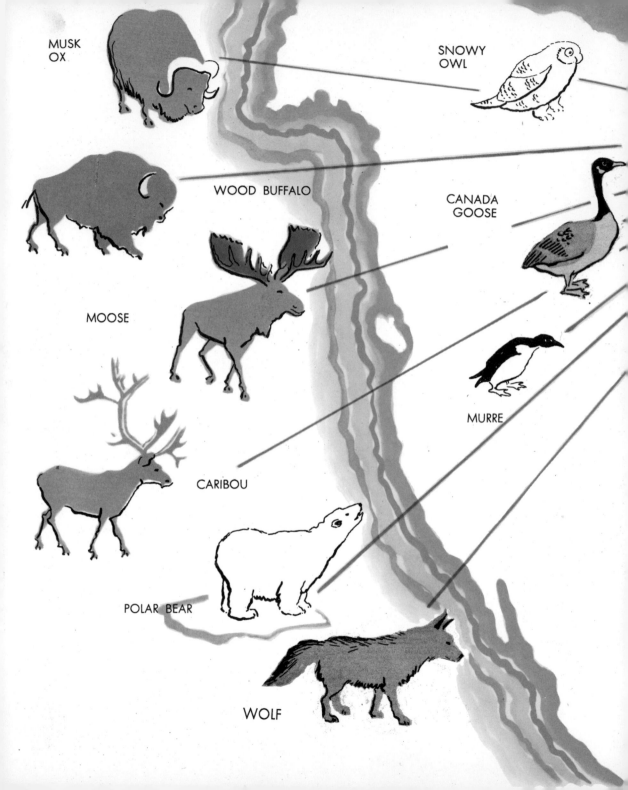

MUSK OX

SNOWY OWL

WOOD BUFFALO

CANADA GOOSE

MOOSE

MURRE

CARIBOU

POLAR BEAR

WOLF

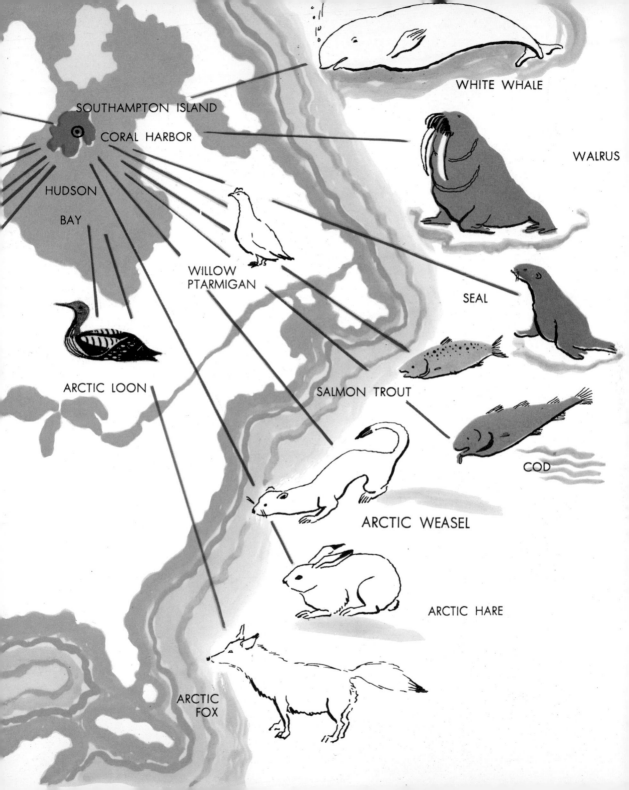

WHITE WHALE

WALRUS

SOUTHAMPTON ISLAND

CORAL HARBOR

HUDSON

BAY

SEAL

WILLOW
PTARMIGAN

SALMON TROUT

ARCTIC LOON

COD

ARCTIC WEASEL

ARCTIC HARE

ARCTIC
FOX